# PUCKSTER GOES TO THE OLYMPICS

BY LORNA SCHULTZ NICHOLSON
ILLUSTRATED BY KELLY FINDLEY

"Have fun, Puckster!"

Puckster's teammates hugged him good-bye. It was time for him to board the plane. He was going to be Team Canada's stick boy at the Winter Olympics!

"Did you pack your surprise?" Charlie asked.

Puckster nodded with a smile. All his teammates knew about the surprise he had in his luggage.

The plane ride was very long. Puckster ate lunch and dinner on the plane.
When night-time came, he stretched out in his seat and tried to sleep. He dreamed he was playing hockey for Team Canada with Sidney Crosby and Rick Nash.

The plane bumped along the runway as it landed.

Puckster helped the team's equipment manager collect the luggage and carry all the hockey sticks to the team bus.

This was Puckster's first time in another country. The bus driver spoke a language that he didn't understand.

The next day, Puckster arrived at the arena and stared up at the waving flags on the roof. They were from different countries and were all different colours. Many people were walking around wearing tracksuits with the name of their country on the back.

At Team Canada's first practice, Puckster handed a stick to every player who stepped on the ice. There was one stick left over.

"That's your stick," said Duncan Keith.

"Mine?" asked Puckster.

"You're practising with us," Duncan said. "We need a spare player." He winked at Puckster.

Puckster ran into the dressing room and quickly put on his equipment.

He stepped on the ice just as Jonathan Toews and Patrice Bergeron whizzed by him. He had a hard time keeping up with the passing and shooting drills. Shea Weber stole the puck from him many times.

Puckster skated with Team Canada at every practice, and each time he became more confident and improved a little.

Finally, the big day came. Team Canada was set to play their first game, and it was against Sweden. The Swedish team wore bright yellow and blue jerseys.

Puckster stared up at all the fans. He didn't bring his surprise today. He wanted to wait.

Puckster stuck his paws in the air and yelled, "Go, Canada, go!" When the Canadian fans heard him, they yelled too. Soon the arena was rocking with noise.

The game started and Canada won the puck. The players rushed up and down the ice and banged against the boards. Puckster watched from beside the bench. He wished he could skate like them.

The game was scoreless until Sweden's Daniel Sedin scored late in the third period. "It's okay!" yelled Puckster.

Team Canada worked hard, but their shots hit the post and crossbar. The ping of the shots echoed through the arena.

When the final buzzer sounded, the score was 1-0 for Sweden.

The next day, Puckster read in the newspaper that many Canadians were angry at Team Canada for losing. It made him feel sad. The players had worked hard.

At the next practice, Sidney Crosby skated over to Puckster.

"Your skating is improving," he said.

"Thanks," said Puckster shyly.

Sidney patted Puckster on the shoulder. "Don't worry about Team Canada. We believe we can win. Just keep cheering!"

Team Canada played Team USA in their second game. Team USA wore red, white, and blue jerseys.

It still wasn't time for his surprise, but Puckster had made a big sign for this game. He jumped up and down and waved his Team Canada sign. He cupped his paws around his mouth and yelled, "Go, Canada, go!"

The crowd roared to life.

13 🍁

When Jonathan Toews scored for Canada, Puckster faced the crowd, pumped his arms in the air, and yelled, "Go, Canada, go!" The fans clapped and chanted, "Can-a-da!"

The score remained 1-0 for Team Canada until Zach Parise scored for Team USA on a breakaway, late in the third period. "It's okay, Canada!" Puckster yelled. "You can get it back!"

The game ended in a tie. As the Team Canada players came off the ice, Puckster patted their backs. "Good game," he said.

"Thanks for cheering, Puckster!" said Rick Nash.

"*Merci beaucoup!*" said Patrice Bergeron with a smile.

My job is more than being a stick boy, Puckster thought. I'm Team Canada's biggest fan. He shivered with excitement. He still had his big surprise.

15 🍁

Every time Puckster practised with the team, he wondered if one day he could play for Team Canada at the Olympics. He had to believe he could so he listened carefully to the coaches and pushed himself to skate faster.

At every game, Puckster got the crowd cheering by doing crazy things. When Team Canada played the Czech Republic, he ran up and down the aisles. Team Canada won that game. When they played Finland, Puckster made up a hip-hop dance. They won that game, too.

Team Canada won the rest of their games. This meant they would be playing in the gold medal game against Russia!

"Puckster, you helped us get to the final," Shea Weber said on the day of the big game. "We couldn't have done it without our fans."

Puckster beamed. He was glad he had saved his surprise for *this* game.

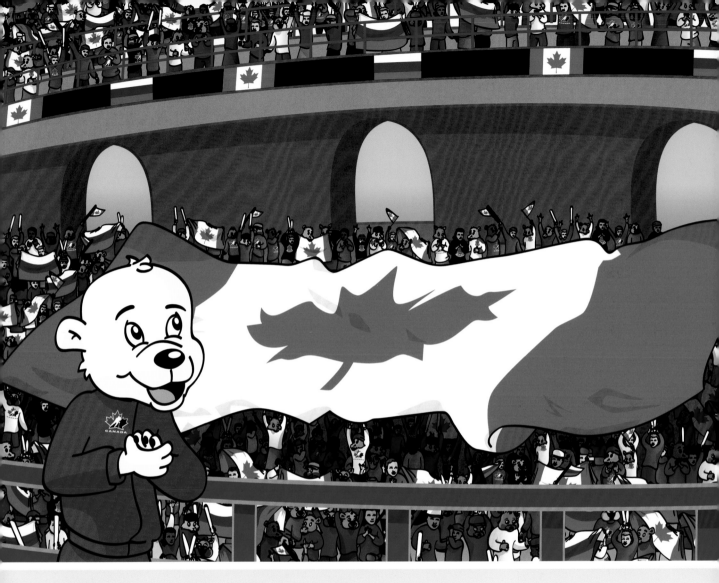

Before the gold medal game, Puckster lined up the sticks and filled the water bottles.

When he finished, he pulled out the surprise from his hockey bag. It was a *gigantic* Canadian flag. Puckster passed it to the fans, and they spread it out over their heads. It covered a whole section of the arena.

The flag made the fans cheer louder than ever: "Go, Canada, go!"

At the end of the first period, the score was 0-0. After two periods, there was still no score. Halfway through the third period, there was a loud crunch against the boards. The arena went silent, and the crowd watched as Jonathan Toews limped off the ice.

"Oh, no," whispered Puckster. "He hurt his knee."

"Puckster!" yelled the coach. "We need you on the bench."

Puckster froze. He worried he wasn't good enough.

"Believe," said Duncan Keith.

Puckster ran to the dressing room and got into his hockey gear. He took his place on the bench. His legs shook. His heart raced.

When it was his turn to play, he jumped over the boards and heard the cheering fans. "Go, Canada, go!"

Puckster skated hard up and down the ice. To his surprise, he kept up with the rest of the players, and he even stopped a scoring chance! All of his practising had paid off.

With a minute left in the game, the score was still 0-0. Puckster watched from the bench. He held his breath.

Jonathan Toews returned to the game for the final shift. He received a pass from Rick Nash and knew he had to act fast. Jonathan saw Sidney Crosby making a break for open ice so he sent him a perfect pass. Sidney raced over the Russian blue line with the puck and fired an incredible slap shot. The puck sank to the back of Russia's net just as the final buzzer rang.

Canada won the gold medal!

All the players jumped over the boards. "Come on, Puckster!" yelled Patrice Bergeron. Puckster hopped over the boards and threw his gloves in the air. The crowd cheered even louder!

With a gold medal around his neck, Puckster looked to the fans and waved. They held up the gigantic Canadian flag that he'd brought to the rink.

"Hooray for Canada! Hooray for Puckster!"

Puckster laughed. He'd brought a surprise with him to the Olympics, but in the end, the surprise had been on him. He'd won a gold medal playing for Team Canada!

**PUCKSTER'S TIPS:**

When sitting on the bench, you should always be ready to play.

Encourage your teammates.

Practice, practice, practice! This applies to everything you do.

**PUCKSTER'S HOCKEY TIP:**

When you are skating, **bend your knees** and **use the muscles in your legs**. Once you pick up speed, make sure you **fully extend your legs** on your stride.

Good luck!